179 DEGREES FROM NOW

Four Stories from Just Past the Edge

By

Thomas Watson

179 Degrees from Now
Four Stories From Just Past the Edge
by Thomas Watson
Copyright October 2017
All Rights Reserved

"A Friend of Kim's"
"Crossing the Pond"
"Page Turner"
"Evidence of Things"

Including excerpts from the novels
The Luck of Han'anga (copyright 2012)
and
The Gryphon Stone (copyright 2017)

 **DESERT STARS PUBLISHING**

This is a work of fantasy. People, places, and things in these stories are either the products of the author's fevered imagination, or reflections of an alternate reality. Any resemblance to actual persons, living or dead, is purely coincidental. Except maybe for the dead ones. You just never know about them, these days.

Other books by this author:

Chance Encounters – Three Short Stories

War of the Second Iteration

The Luck of Han'anga
Founders' Effect
The Plight of the Eli'ahtna
The Courage to Accept
Setha'im Prosh

Nonfiction: (Amateur Astronomy)

Mr. Olcott's Skies
Tales of a Three-legged Newt

CONTENTS

	Acknowledgments	i
1	A Friend of Kim's	1
2	Crossing the Pond	18
3	Page Turner	29
4	Evidence of Things	40
	Excerpt from The Luck of Han'anga	56
	Excerpt from The Gryphon Stone	62

With thanks to John Hindmarsh and Paul Alan Piatt for their help in making these stories work, and to Steven Howser, Ron Boe, and Linda Watson for last minute proof reading.

A FRIEND OF KIM'S

"She's too old for this imaginary friend nonsense," said George.

"We're concerned this will keep her from making *real* friends," Delores added. "She needs to outgrow this business and be more engaged with the real world."

"Real people," George added.

"Oh, I understand," Rick assured Kim's parents. "No more saying hello to Katie, asking her how she is, or anything of the sort."

"Definitely don't pretend that you hear her speak," said Delores.

"Not any more. I was just, you know, being nice to Kim."

"Oh, we know," George assured him with a genuine smile on his round, good-natured face.

"And we knew you'd understand where we were coming from."

"Oh, I do understand. Don't worry about it. I've got this."

"Thanks, Rick." Delores sounded relieved.

Their request put Rick in an awkward spot, but there was nothing for it. He needed to make it work. Rick was, in fact, well-motivated. He liked these people, cared about them, and wanted to do well by them. Needed to do well. He was in love with their older daughter Irene and planned to marry her. That was likely to get complicated enough, if Irene said yes, so he saw no need to risk alienating her folks. Last time he and his friend Matt had kicked back and had a beer together, Matt had guessed that Rick, George, and Delores would soon have "the talk" regarding their younger daughter. His advice had been to go along with it and, Matt being something of an expert in such matters, Rick trusted that advice.

And he followed it, leaving one less thing to chance. Rick was pretty sure Irene would not be completely surprised when he offered her the ring in his pocket, but that didn't guarantee a positive answer. She'd been through a lot, he knew; a really bad time before they'd met. Living with her folks had been part of her fallback. Rick fought the urge to keep putting his hand in his jacket pocket to make sure the ring was there. He was also reasonably confident that her folks would be pleased – if she said yes. George and Delores had long since accepted him as one of the family. All that remained was Irene agreeing to make it official.

So Rick smiled and nodded and agreed, and when the parents were elsewhere in the house and Kimberly was left to entertain him while waiting for Irene, they had a quick, quiet talk about the matter.

"Oh," said Kim, managing to look downcast and self-conscious at the same time.

"Hey," and Rick put a finger under her chin and made her look at him where he sat. "You know better. But we have to play along, okay?" He tousled her fair hair. "When it's just us, it'll be like it was before. When your mom and dad and sister are around, we go into stealth mode."

A smile lit the pixie face of his small friend. And she really was, small and slim for a seven-year-old girl. And almost scary smart. "Stealth mode! That sounds sneaky!"

"It is," Rick assured her

Looking around carefully, Kim whispered, "Katie knows why you're here!"

"Does she, now?" Rick grinned down at the kid and lowered his voice. "Promise not to say anything?" He shifted his gaze to his right. "Both of you?"

"We promise!" Giggles ensued.

"What do you think about it?"

Kim gave him a cheesy grin and said, "We think it's gonna be cool!"

"I think you're right... Uh, oh... Stealth mode!"

Kim turned part way to her left and made a quick shushing sound, and a moment later Delores was in the living room from the kitchen. "Rick, you certainly look handsome tonight. You must have quite an evening planned."

"Well – thanks. Birthdays are special," he replied.

Delores looked from him to Kim and back when her youngest child made a tiny sound. A maternal eyebrow was raised. "Okay, what are you two up to?"

"Nothing!" Kim asserted just a bit too quickly.

"Don't look at me," Rick said.

Delores chuckled and shook her head. "What is keeping that girl? I'll go check on her." She headed down the hall.

"You guys are a lot of help," Rick muttered.

"It was Katie! She poked me."

"Yes, she did. And I saw her do it." Rick tousled her hair again, then made the same gesture beside her, with a wink and a grin.

Kim grinned back and said quietly, "She says that tickles!"

"Good! It's supposed to. And no, I don't know why Kim keeps repeating everything you say."

Eye rolling was followed by more giggling. "Stealth!"

Kim was suddenly ever so nonchalant.

Irene appeared at the end of the hall at that moment, paused, and turned around once. "Well, what do you think?"

"I think someone brought Audrey Hepburn back to life." It was corny as hell, and he was grinning like a fool, but damned if Irene didn't look the part with her short, dark hair and in that sleeveless black dress. The wonder of it, that this amazing woman had fallen for him, for a moment robbed him of the ability to speak. The feeling slammed face-first into his self-image of being just an average sort of guy. Women this intelligent and beautiful did *not* settle for average guys, and yet here she was. Giving him that look.

Irene laughed and came to him, taking his hands and giving him a quick kiss. He could swear she was sparkling. Matt would think he'd lost his mind, and likely not blame him for it in the slightest.

"Happy birthday."

"Thanks!"

With a quick glance at Delores and down to Kim, Rick said, "And we need to take off. They don't hold reservations where we're going."

"And you won't give me even the tiniest clue about where that is?" Irene teased.

"Nope."

"Well, then..." Irene picked up a couple of items from the back of the sofa, a miniscule handbag and a short black jacket. "It's a warm evening, but most restaurants let it get too chilly inside." She held her hand out to him and he took it, leading her to the door.

"When do you expect to be back?" Delores asked.

Irene gave her a look and a raised eyebrow, and her mother struggled to keep a straight face.

"Have fun!" Delores said. And gave Rick a wink.

Outside, Rick said, "I doubt I'll ever get used to that."

"Get used to what?" Irene asked.

"Your mother being so, um, accepting of our relationship."

"Meaning the fact that I spend more and more of my time in your apartment?"

Rick laughed as he opened the passenger door of the car. "Your father asked me if we were planning to move in together any time soon!"

"Oh, gawd! He didn't!"

"Afraid so." Rick paused, then added, "He seemed sort of – wary, the way he said it."

Nothing more was said for a moment as she got in, and he went around to the driver's side and sat down. "You know why he asked that." It wasn't a question.

Rick nodded and started his car. "Yes, I can figure it out, from what you told me about your ex. And I can't blame him for being concerned."

"It was – not a good time. But I've moved on." She nodded a little as she spoke. "And my father knows you'd never hurt me."

"He's right about that." The engine came quietly to life, and he turned toward her, reaching over to squeeze her hand, feeling again the pang of fear over how she'd respond to a marriage proposal after having survived an abusive relationship. There was trust between them, but how much could it take? "None of that tonight. Birthday, remember?"

"Right." Irene squeezed his hand and her smile brightened.

There was so often a shadow behind her smile. He didn't see any at the moment, and it gave him a warm feeling, knowing why.

Rick drove his nice but unpretentious car from her parent's home, tucked away in a bedroom community in the hills, down into the bright lights of the big city. They arrived in plenty of time for the reservation, and Irene was beautifully surprised by the place he'd chosen, exactly as Rick hoped. They drank and danced and laughed, and looked into each other's eyes as lovers do. Rick couldn't help noticing people glancing their way with knowing smiles.

Matt held to his promise not to crash the party.

The night was no longer young when they decided it was time for a change in venue. Rick suggested a modest detour on the way to his apartment, Irene having made it quite plain through comments whispered in his ear that the party wasn't going to end with dinner and dancing. He didn't specifically say why he wanted to stop at a particular spot in the hills, overlooking the city. There was no need. It was a place they thought of as their own, a place for quiet conversations and quieter moments, and there was nothing unusual about going there after a date. He drove away from the city and back into the hills, leaving the lights and noise behind once again, and in time they came to that special spot and pulled over. Below them sprawled a sea of lights that filled the valley.

Before Rick could form the right words, Irene had a question. "Should we move in together?"

"Yes," he replied.

"Yes? Just yes?"

"Were you expecting an argument?" He smiled at her, brushing her cheek gently with his fingertips. She ducked her head against his hand and closed her eyes. "After all, married couples generally live at the same address."

As he fished the little box out of his pocket, she looked up, eyes open wide and dark in the low light spilling up from the valley. "Married...?" in a small voice. Irene stared at the small box as he opened it and revealed its contents. "Rick – are you sure about this?"

"Never been more sure in my life." Rick was astonished by how clearly and easily the words came out. "Will you marry me?"

Irene looked up at him again and, just as clearly, said, "Yes. I will."

Rick slipped the ring on her finger. It was no gigantic rock, to be sure, but it clearly pleased her no end. He avoided saying anything stupid, then, as if he should make apologies for the ring's modesty. He knew she was better than that.

"Rick..." She put her arms around his neck and pulled him to her. They kissed for a long time, and he only broke from her in that moment when he realized they weren't alone.

There was someone in the car with them.

"Go home! Go home!"

They both jumped violently and twisted around to look in the back seat, from whence came that shrill demand. There was a little girl sitting there, wearing a plain, white dress, terror in her wide, dark eyes, which were fastened on Irene. "Please, go home!" she implored. *"Go home now!"*

Rick couldn't help himself. "Katie?" The name blurted out.

The little girl wasn't there anymore.

Rick disentangled himself from Irene and started the car. With a squeal of rubber on pavement, he sent them roaring back onto the road.

"Rick, what's going on?" There was fear in her voice that echoed his own sudden anxiety.

"We're going back to your house, as quick as we can," he replied.

"Who was that? Where did she go?" There was a pause as she gasped when he took a curve too quickly. "You said – Katie?"

There was nothing for it. "Yes, that was Katie. Your sister's friend." Another curve too fast, and Rick fought to stay in control of both himself and the vehicle. They wouldn't be able to help anyone if he wrecked the car.

"But she's..." Irene was staring ahead, gripping the dashboard with both hands. "She's..."

"Not real?" Rick finished, not so much as glancing away from the road. "It's not that simple. Katie is, well, her own sort of reality. One that normally only someone like Kim can see."

"What do you mean by that?" Irene sounded puzzled and wary, all at once.

"Kim can see further than most. She can see Katie's reality. Well, part of it, anyway. That's why they bonded." He moderated his speed as they started passing more houses, dark shapes on hillsides with embedded lights, gone in an eye blink.

"I don't understand!"

"I'll try to explain later," Rick promised.

"Rick – God, I'm scared. I don't know what to think!" She drew a gasping breath. "I mean, I saw that girl! And then she was just – gone!"

"I'm scared too. Katie wouldn't manifest in that way without a compelling reason." He sped up and just made the first traffic light they encountered. Fortunately, it was very late, and traffic was almost nonexistent. "It's really hard for them, almost impossible. That she felt the need... Something's wrong!"

Irene opened her small, black handbag and pulled out her phone. She tapped the phone and paused, then said, "Hello! Someone pick up, please. It's Irene. Hello?" She waited, but there was no response. "Rick, they should have answered. They weren't going anywhere tonight. Someone should have answered! Oh, my God, should I call the police?"

"What would we tell them? Wait! Any of the neighbors on your contact list?"

"Yes!" She swiped and tapped at the phone, then said, "Mildred? It's Irene from across the street. I'm out with Rick and, well, would you mind going over to my folks' house and ringing the doorbell? They, uh – well, they were supposed call me and when they didn't and I called them, nobody answered. They should be home. Getting a bit worried." There was a pause, then, "Thanks!"

"We're about five minutes away," Rick muttered half to himself. "Damn, that's going to be a long five minutes!"

"Rick?" He risked a glance and saw her staring at him, clutching her phone like a talisman. "How do you know all this? You – were you like Kim?"

"Yes." It was enough of the truth for the moment. "We're almost there."

There was another question, an inevitable question. Rick could almost see the words being shaped on her lips. She didn't have a chance to ask it. They came around a corner, and into her neighborhood. Ahead and to the left was a dull, warm glow that flickered. And a crowd in the street, with more people running toward the scene.

"Oh, no! *Oh, no!*" It was a scream the second time, and Irene had dropped her phone and was clutching the dashboard again.

Rick aimed for a spot along the side of the road short of the crowd and pulled over in a less-than-perfect parking maneuver that bounced them around in the car a bit. Irene was out and running as fast as her insensible shoes would allow. Rick caught up with her in a moment and sprinted past. There were no lights on in the house, unless he counted the glow of the fire showing through the front bedroom windows. Smoke poured out from under the roof in several places. Irene was screaming; Rick looked over his shoulder and saw her trying to break free from a man and woman holding her back. The woman was Delores. The man was *not* George.

"They're in there!" Irene was screaming.

"You can't!" Delores shouted. "You can't!"

He didn't slow down, though someone tried to catch his arm. From somewhere he could hear sirens, but something in his gut said waiting would be wrong, just wrong. Rick hit the door and heard the wood around the hinges crack. He gathered himself for another rush.

"On three!" Matt shouted, and counted, and they hurled themselves at the door, which shattered under their combined weight. Rick dropped to the floor, below the worst of the smoke, Matt beside him, dressed in jeans and a brown blazer, and not a hair out of place. The smoke detector in the hallway screamed a useless warning. "Katie says the kids are in Kim's bedroom. George is in his office. I'll get the girls!"

They crawled down the hall together at first, then Rick made a left through the door to the room George used for a home office. Matt disappeared into the shadows and smoke, casting no shadow of his own though he was silhouetted by the pulsing glow coming from the rec room. The fire was there, licking out as if feeding on the wavy curls of smoke rolling under the ceiling. It was spreading swiftly; he could almost feel it gather to spring like some wild animal. Rick started coughing. The heat and smoke were stealing his breath.

There was George, sprawled on the floor in sweats and a bathrobe. No sign of life. Rick started dragging George, trying to remain in the clearer, but still tainted lower air. It was no good. He'd never get both of them out in time that way. With a gasping breath he filled his lungs, held it, and staggered to his feet with George in a classic fireman's carry. Lurching and almost falling with every step, he stumped down the hall toward the front room and the door.

"Right behind you, Ricky! We're good."

Rick didn't dare reply, with his head in the smoke and his eyes stinging. They made it to the door and staggered out, and there were firefighters rushing up the walk toward them, backlit by flashing blue and red lights, washed out by a bright white glare. Even as Rick noted this, the house behind him erupted in a muffled *whump* and a blast of heat hit him from behind.

He would have fallen, but the firefighters were there, catching him, hauling him away from danger, taking the burden from his shoulders and sweeping Kim up and away. A whirl of confusion spun him about as others rushed by and water seemed to pour from nowhere onto the house and into the house. Rick lost himself in the flashing lights and smoke and steam and a babble of voices.

Rick found himself sitting on the end of an ambulance, with someone holding a mask over his face telling him to breathe deeply and slowly. He nodded and did so, and what went into his lungs was cool and pure. He coughed a couple of times, then cleared his throat and after a few minutes found he could breathe easily. Rick looked into the eyes of the paramedic crouched beside him and nodded.

"Looks like you'll be okay," she said, patting his shoulder. "You should go to the hospital with the others and get checked out, though, just to be safe. That was nice work, by the way."

"Thanks." The paramedic disappeared around the side of the vehicle, and Rick looked for Irene and her family. Near the back end of another ambulance, Delores was bent over a gurney as the crew prepared to move it inside. George was strapped to it. Delores had George's hand between hers and was talking to him, but Rick couldn't hear what she said. To his relief he saw an oxygen mask over George's nose and mouth jiggle as he nodded in response to something she said. The paramedics hovering over him weren't doing anything other than lining the gurney up. No CPR, nothing to indicate George was in immediate danger.

Not far from her parents, Irene stood with Kim. The sisters were surrounded by neighbors who's faces ranged from stunned to concerned. Matt stood behind Irene and Katie was there holding Kim's hand. Matt gave him a grin and a wink, then he and Katie were gone. Rick waved a hand at Irene when her father was loaded and the ambulance door closed. The sisters came to him at a trot, their mother trailing along behind. A moment later all three were clinging to him; they were all crying.

Delores caught her breath first. Seeing this, Rick said, "George?"

"They said he was stable," she replied, sniffling a bit. "They don't know yet what happened to him."

"Our house is all burned up, isn't it?" Kim said.

"Looks pretty bad," he admitted. "Let's wait and see, huh? What happened? Do you know?" Kim shook her head. "Are you okay?"

Kim gave him a nod. "Katie helped me."

"Why didn't you run outside?" he asked.

Kim shrugged and said, "I got scared!"

"They're taking George away to the hospital," Delores said. "Mildred will drive us over."

With a glance at Irene, Rick said, "We'll follow in my car." Delores nodded and, leading Kim by the hand, walked into the thinning crowd toward a short, grey-haired woman who was clearly waiting for them. The paramedic reappeared and suggested that Irene do the driving. As they walked back toward his car,

Rick felt the quivering of reaction begin, and decided it was a good idea. He gave Irene the keys. In the car, she put the key into the ignition, then looked at her parents' house. The fire was all but out, and steam rose pale into the night. She turned toward him.

"You weren't alone when you went in, were you?"

"No," Rick shook his head, his words heavy and reluctant. Even if she believed him, the strangeness of it all would probably change everything for her. And this, after all she'd been though before. He feared the consequences of those changes. How could she trust him now, with such strangeness in his life? "My friend Matt was with me. He got to Kim and Katie. I went for your father."

"When you hit the door the second time, it was like a battering ram crushed it!"

"Matt's a big guy."

"When you came out..." Irene hesitated. "You were carrying my Dad like he weighed nothing."

"Oh, he was damned heavy, believe me! But Matt was giving me an assist by then. Like at the door." Rick slumped back in the car seat. "Damn it, Matt and I had things worked out so you'd never need to know about any of this!"

"Is he here, with us, now?"

"No," Rick assured her. "We have an agreement. You – believe what I'm telling you?"

"I believe what I saw, what I *felt*, but I have no idea what to do or say or think," she whispered, looking at the ring she wore. "An hour ago, I was as happy as I've ever been. And now – God! What is all of this?"

"I understand," Rick said, his heart sinking like a stone. "It's going to take time, and a lot of explaining, and if you don't want to..."

"Will our kids be like you?" she blurted out. She looked at him, eyes wide in the dark. "Will they have – friends?" Irene stumbled over that last word.

"I don't know." He couldn't take his voice above a whisper. Hope soared in him, but he didn't dare smile or say much more. "Maybe."

Irene stared at him for a moment that stretched just long enough for hope to falter. Then she leaned forward and kissed him gently. "We should get going. They'll worry." She put the car into gear and pulled away from the curb, edging slowly past the emergency vehicles that still crowded the road.

Relief flooded through his worry, though the worry still remained. It wasn't going to be as easy as all that, he was sure. But...

Their children – *she* had said that. Hope took a firmer grip on his heart as they drove along. It was going to be complicated, for sure, but maybe their children *would* have friends of that sort. Rick hoped so.

It was good to have friends, after all.

CROSSING THE POND

As she paused for a moment, outside the rectangle of bare ground marked by short stone posts, Sam realized she'd never seen her friend step into that patch of well-trodden ground. They'd walked the path around the pond many times during their long friendship, at least once a year since the annual conference had been established in Concord. That was a lot of years back.

Wait, Sam thought. *I've never done it either.* Unable to think of a single reason not to, Sam stepped through the gap between the two posts that lacked a curved cable between them. Past the solitary stone with the message declaring that this was the place, the very spot on which the cabin once stood.

"There!" said Sam, feeling foolish, but not at all displeased. She smiled back at Malcolm in the wake of those impulsive steps. "Finally."

"Oh, come on, Sam," Malcolm said with a laugh and a bright smile on his round, dark face. "No one has ever convinced me that's really the exact spot."

"Near enough as no matter?" Sam asked, stepping back between the posts. "There's a very good chance they're right, you know. The evidence is pretty solid. In which case, there I was."

Malcolm shrugged. "A few feet, more or less. It was surely somewhere nearby. A few steps to what used to be, such a long time ago."

His smile was replaced by a wistful look that seemed in keeping with the grey, damp autumn afternoon around them. "You keep doing that," Sam said when she saw the change.

"Doing what?"

"Going distant and melancholy." Sam came closer and looked Malcolm in the eyes. "What's up, old friend? What's bothering you?"

Malcolm chuckled and tapped the side of his head. "Writing," he said. "A new essay is coming to life."

"No, that's a different sort of distraction. I know, I've seen it often enough!"

He shook his head and the wistful look faded into one of weariness. Malcolm took a deep breath and released it with a sigh, looking like a man about to make a confession. "It's nothing. I'm just a little tired. The flights to these meetings are harder on me every year, especially with all the delays and extra security hassles. To say nothing of being surrounded by people whining about the hassles. It gets old quickly."

"Which?" Sam asked.

"All of it, but especially the whining." Malcolm grimaced. "Honestly, if people had acted this way at the start of the Second World War, we'd be speaking German. Those of us allowed to speak at all."

"Probably right," Sam replied as they started walking the path again. The sky was a duller grey, and the clouds were lower. "There's a good chance we're going to be rained on, this time."

Malcolm looked up at the sky. "No, my shoulder doesn't ache." He looked down at Sam and smiled a little. "Not until later tonight, I'm guessing."

"No guess," Sam said. "I watch the weather news, too, you know." Sniffing the still, wet air, she added, "I'm thinking they've got it wrong this time."

"Maybe."

"Seriously, what's bothering you?"

Malcolm glanced sidelong at his companion, then looked ahead, saying nothing for a several yards and moments. Ahead was a bench that faced the water, overlooking a short stretch of bare shoreline. The woods came very near the shore, and in other seasons would be green and leafy. Most of the trees were bare, with a few oaks reluctant to shed brown dead leaves, and a single evergreen that defied the approach of winter. Thin, fading grass surround the bench, almost down to the water, struggling to live in soil compacted by many thousands of footfalls over the years. "Let's have a seat," he said.

They'd rested and talked on that bench many times. On this occasion they sat for a while in companionable silence, watching the calm, smooth surface of Walden Pond. The far shore was hazy, and the trees across the way blended into a rough, dark band that did not resolve into individual plants. As Sam watched, the haze thickened into a bank of fog, a soft grey layer with the dark crowns of trees on top, and pewter waters below. Sam wished for a camera; it was a lovely, if melancholy, sight.

"So?" Sam prompted.

Another deep sigh escaped Malcolm and he sagged a bit, as if accepting a great burden. "I don't have much time left, Sam."

"What do you mean?" Though of course Sam knew enough about her friend's condition to guess. That guess turned her heart to a heavy stone.

"I'm no longer responding to the treatments." Malcolm turned to Sam and shrugged. "In fact, they've become counterproductive. So I've ended them."

"Ah, damn!" Sam leaned forward, head bowed by the weight of impending grief. "Do they know how long?"

Shaking his head, Malcolm said, "Not really. A few weeks before pain medications aren't enough. After that, who knows? Could be weeks. Could be months. The latter, if it's just the cancer. But my heart isn't one hundred percent, and the treatments really messed up my kidneys."

"Damn," Sam muttered again.

"Ah, now," Malcolm said, setting his arm around Sam's shoulders. "We've both known all along it would come to this. That's why they talk about survival, and not cures, with this one."

"You were doing so well, for so long," Now it was Sam's turn for a deep breath and a sigh. "I suppose I managed to forget that. Does Bernie know?"

"Yes, she does."

"And let you come all this way?"

Malcolm actually laughed. "Why do you think she came along, this time?"

"Ah, well, it wasn't entirely without precedent," Sam replied. "But you're right, that should have made me wonder." She felt the clouds dropping lower, but upon glancing up realized it was an illusion born of her mood.

Silence surrounded them again as they sat, each with an arm around the other. Not a breath of air stirred. Life seemed to have retreated from the pond, leaving them entirely alone. The fog over the pond was thicker and nearer, and only the tips of the tallest trees on the far shore dotted the upper edge of the fog bank. They faded from sight one by one, and the bank became a wall. From that silence, the realization came to Sam that they truly had the place to themselves. An unusual occurrence, considering where they were, beside the body of water that gave its name to one of the most famous works of all American literature. There was usually someone strolling this path, no matter the weather, seeking inspiration or illumination.

Just as well, thought Sam. *Yes, just as well we're alone.*

"At the moment," Malcolm's voice seemed loud and sudden coming into the grey silence around them. "At the moment, I don't feel ill at all. I'm a bit tired, but after that flight just about anyone would be. And in this moment, it's very hard to believe the end is near."

"Well, it isn't exactly knocking on the door," Sam pointed out.

"Not from what I'm told," Malcolm agreed. "But I can't help wondering. Are doctors really any better at predicting things than the folks at the weather service?" He held out his hand and looked up at the featureless clouds. "I do believe it's begun to rain!"

Malcolm was right, though the scattered drops didn't come down for very long. This was a relief to Sam, since Malcolm showed no sign he intended to get up and seek shelter. The smooth surface of the pond was speckled for only a few minutes, and slender rings raced out from each impact. The rings met, overlapped, interfered, and faded away. The pond was still once more.

The fog encroached upon their position. Sam could only see the water a few yards from where they sat before it faded into the veil. As humid as it was, it seemed odd to Sam that they were not damp from dew or the brief rain that had fallen.

"I was about to utter something inane about having no regrets," Malcolm said with a quiet laugh. "Is there a human being on this planet who can say so and not be just a little dishonest?"

"You have regrets?"

"Oh, one or two," Malcolm replied. "But none of them are things I could have prevented, and I can't change any of it now." He smiled again, seemingly at ease. "There certainly were some things I'd change, that's for damned sure!"

"It should have been less of a struggle to make your way into academia," Sam said.

"Yes, I quite agree. But I persisted, and I had good people on my side." Malcolm turned toward Sam and smiled. His face looked suddenly youthful, an illusion hampered by the amount of grey in his hair. "I've seen such changes, Sam. No, the world isn't perfect and we have a lot to learn, still. My God, so much to do! But..." He took Sam's hand, holding it up between them, a dark strong hand clasping a slender white one. "When I was a boy, they'd have strung me up for this. Just this!" He chuckled and let go. "But here we sit, together. Oh, we have a long damned way to go. But that doesn't mean we haven't come a long way. Mustn't forget that!"

"You certainly went a long way," Sam said. "And for good reason. No one reads or discusses Thoreau like you. When you read, people *understand*."

At that, Malcolm laughed aloud. "Well, I wish they'd explain it to *me* then, sometime!"

Looking at Malcolm, Sam thought, *Yes, it is hard to believe. Almost impossible. He's so alive right now!*

It would only become harder to believe, Sam was sure. Much harder.

"I especially don't regret meeting you, old friend," Malcolm said with a grin. "That was surely the major turning point in my career! It was the two of us together getting the ball rolling that made the conference..." He stopped speaking and peered ahead into the fog. "What on earth was that? Did you hear? Are you hearing it now?"

"I hear something," Sam replied, puzzled. The sound was difficult to sort out, as if it was heard from a greater distance than the width of Walden Pond. "A bird?"

"I've only heard certain thrushes make a sound that pure," Malcolm replied. "They're long gone by this time of year. Loon?"

"You or me?"

"Be serious!" Malcolm said, even though he turned to Sam and winked. "Do they even come here?"

"Maybe in winter." The plaintive notes drifted from the fog again. "Damned if that doesn't sound like a flute!"

"Out on the water, in that fog?" Malcolm raised an eyebrow.

"Seems to be drifting toward us," Sam observed. They could hear the sounds more clearly, and there was a melody the ear could follow. A simple tune, gentle and repetitive, and it seemed to emerge from the fog as if the fog played the tune, and not some earthly instrument. Sam looked around, realizing the fog had closed in around them. They could just see the water's edge, the bench, and each other. The air was cool and fragrant with the scent of damp autumn woodland, a leaf mold smell that suddenly seemed so right.

There was a boat, an old and weather-beaten rowboat. Sam could see it clearly enough as it nudged the shore, though she hadn't been aware of its approach. A bearded man with unkempt hair stood in the bow. He wore a long coat buttoned all the way to his collarbone, trousers, and boots. All were dark but of indeterminant color, as if the fog robbed them of hue. His face was pale and his expression wistful. In his left hand was a wooden flute.

"Good day, sir," said the man in the boat, which stayed grounded of its own accord.

"And to you as well." Malcolm rose to his feet and said, "It's a pleasure to meet you. Also, something of a surprise."

"Is it now? A surprise, I mean?"

"Perhaps not," Malcolm replied with a quiet laugh.

Sam stood beside her friend, started to reach for his hand, and could not. She had no ability to move at all, and the chill seemed to reach into her, holding her still. The two men facing each other across the bow of the rowboat seemed unaware of her existence.

"Have we not met already, once upon a time?" the boatman asked, waving the flute around to encompass the woods beyond the fog. "Perhaps a very long time ago?"

"Perhaps," Malcolm agreed. "It may have been an ancestor of mine. Or not."

"Ah, what does it matter? We're well-met now!"

"Indeed!"

"We should go." The flute moved to indicate the boat. "The way is long. Just as well, really, for we have much to discuss!"

"Yes," Malcolm said. He turned to Sam and gripped her by her shoulders. "I love you, Samantha. I always have. Remember that. And – help Bernice where you can. This will be hard for her." He leaned forward to kiss her forehead; his lips were strangely warm, as if lit by a fever. She felt the warmth linger as he turned from her.

The boatman extended a hand to steady his passenger as he stepped aboard, and Malcolm clasped it, saying, "Thank you, Henry."

"You are most welcome, my friend." The boatman turned dark eyes toward Sam and said, "We will meet again one day, though not soon!" He winked at her.

The boat slid a way into the fog and vanished in an instant. There was no sound of water, no splash of oars. It simply drifted from the shore and was gone. Sam heard two things just after it vanished. She heard Malcolm laugh in a voice she remembered from younger days. And then the flute played for a moment.

Sam stood alone in a gentle drizzle, cold and wet. The fog was gone and she could see across the pond, but there was no sign of a rowboat, a boatman, or her friend. Groping for the back of the bench to steady herself, she found Malcolm sitting there where he'd been all along. Baffled, she laid a hand on his shoulder, and realized the truth. Suddenly weary and chilled to the bone, she sat heavily on the bench, staring without seeing over Walden Pond. She waited for grief to come.

In its place came the memory of that last laugh, ringing clearly through the fog. There had been such joy in it!

"Ah, Malcolm!" she whispered.

Sam stood up and, seeing two young people approaching under the cover of an umbrella, called to them for help. She wondered what to say to Bernice.

PAGE TURNER

"It's an interesting concept, that business about the landscape of energy levels and tunneling, but it doesn't really work that way."

Try as I might, I couldn't place the man's accent. It was subtle and added to the air of uniqueness that shadowed the stranger. His clothing, dark brown blazer over a white shirt – no tie – and pants, had a style that reminded me of old movies. From the 1960s, maybe. "Forgive me, but I overheard talk of the multiverse as I walked by, and it's an area of special interest for me."

The five of us lounged around a table covered by a dark red cloth. There was an unlit candle in the center, almost hidden by empty beer bottles. The white noise of overlapping conversations ebbed and flowed around us as other convention attendees celebrated the first evening of this gathering. We were both fans and practitioners of the genre, all with science backgrounds, though none of us had cut it as scientists. We were knowledgeable, however, and made an effort to keep up. We had indeed been discussing the concept of the multiverse, its possibilities and, because we were all writers, its use in science fiction.

"Really," said Mel, and it didn't quite sound like a question. Of the members of our local author clique, he was the most well-known and yet least approachable by fans. Also, the one most likely to put someone off.

I'm the opposite of Mel, especially when the person in question is good looking. "Are you a researcher?" I asked. "Theorist?"

He was of average height and build, with black hair and grey eyes. I could see Sylvia sizing him up already. He smiled at me and shook his head. "Experimental physics. Though I assure you, I can do the math."

"What brings you to this gathering?" Sylvia asked, flicking a glance my way.

"Curiosity," he replied with a shrug.

I wondered if anyone else noted the slight hesitation before his reply. If so, no one blinked. There were two spare chairs at the table, and Sylvia waved a hand toward one.

"Have a seat and tell us how we're wrong." She definitely had her eyes on him, but at the same time the invitation contained a challenge. Sylvia doesn't much care for being contradicted or corrected. At least, so says her editor.

The smile faded into something rueful, and I thought he was about to back off. You see that happen at gatherings such as this, where fans stick a foot in it and realize they're headed for deep water. Then he laughed and said, "Oh, why not? What harm could it possibly do?" He took the offered chair and sat.

The air of oddity about the man settled into the chair with him. I still couldn't put my finger on it. The way he moved, the sound of his voice, all of it oddly familiar, as if we'd met somewhere before. Déjà vu; I couldn't resist. "Have we met?" I asked, earning brief glare from Sylvia.

"Highly unlikely," he said with a smile. Whatever else, he had a nice smile.

"So," said Mel. "In what way have we erred?"

"Well, from what I overheard you believe the multiverse can best be described in terms of a landscape, with peaks and valleys representing energy gradients and potentialities for tunneling that would generate yet another parallel reality. Unfortunately, if you're looking to travel from one universe to another, that's not helpful. You'd be creating your own destination."

Mel looked thoughtful. I could almost hear ideas clicking together in his head.

James made a tiny strangled noise. Our guest had just summed up in a nutshell, and neatly shot down, about half an hour's worth of conversation between five people who had, half the time, been talking out their asses.

"Okay," said Jenna, who at that point realized the bottle she held was empty. "Um, I'll get the next round." And looking at our guest, raised an eyebrow.

"Yes, thanks," he replied to the unnecessary question.

"Where are you from?" asked James.

"Oh, not too far from here, actually." The stranger in the dark suit had a bemused look to him as he spoke. "Call me – Brian."

You know, for just a moment I thought he was going to say something else.

There followed a round of introductions – myself, Mel, Sylvia, and James – sometimes repeated to make things clear over the noise around us.

"And the one bringing the beer even as we speak is Jenna," I said at the end of that. She'd just come within earshot, having dodged her way through the crowd carrying a tray loaded with beer from the open bar.

"Attendance must be up this year," she said. With very little help from Mel, the beers were distributed. "They're afraid of running out!"

"This thing is only scheduled to run another hour," Mel pointed out. "The herd will thin before then."

Bottles were raised in mutual salute.

"So," said James after taking a drink. "Where did we go wrong?"

"That sort of speculation is too coarse," Brian replied. "The multiverse is more fine-grained. Infinitely so, in fact, with parallel universes of related types packed into layered membrane-like structures."

"I've heard of that," I said. "It's called the brane multiverse."

"I'll bet that lends itself to some very weak cranial jests," Brian said, flashing me a smile.

So, I'm a sucker for a nice smile, and Brian had one. "No bet. I've heard some lame ones."

"That isn't exactly how that multiverse is usually described," Sylvia said, giving me a stern look. I put on an air of presumed innocence.

"Be that as it may," Brian said. "The idea contains some elements of the truth, but a better metaphor would be picture books."

"'Picture books?'" James echoes. "I can't wait to hear this!"

"I can't wait to hear his credentials," Jenna muttered. "No offense."

"None taken, and all in good time." Brian sipped his beer and smiled, looking for a moment rather wistful. Then his eyes focused on us and he began. "Imagine that the multiverse is an infinitely large collection of books, each book the equivalent of a brane. Each volume contains an infinite number of pages, each a picture that represents a universe."

"Ah, the invocation of infinity!" Mel said with a sarcastic laugh. "Solves a host of speculative ills."

"Doesn't it though?" Brian responded with a smirk, clearly unfazed by Mel's attitude. "Well, imagine it all the same, though if you claim the ability to imagine infinity you're either some sort of god or a liar."

"Somewhere in the middle," James said, raising his beer in a mock salute. "We're writers!"

Brian looked around at the crowded tables and the shifting crowd. "So this is some sort of literary gathering?"

"Science fiction convention," I said.

"Ah, that would explain why some of the folks I saw earlier looked like they weren't from around here!" His eyes tracked a young man dressed as an otherworldly character in a popular TV series.

"In a way very few of them are from around here," Mel said. He tapped the side of his head and rolled his eyes.

"Do tell," Brian muttered, just before taking a swig of beer. "Well, pick a brane..."

"We're picking yours at the moment," Sylvia said.

"Another lame brane joke," I muttered. Everyone groaned except Sylvia and Brian. The latter gave me a wink, the former a glare.

"This one will do," Brian continued. "It's part of an infinite continuum of parallel realities. Those closest to it are so similar that if you could travel from one to the other, it would be impossible to tell you'd accomplished anything at all. You'd need to flip through a great many pages to see that the picture had changed much, enough that you could honestly say you were somewhere else."

"And the other branes?" asked James.

"Well, each brane holds universes that have certain parameters in common," Brian replied. "Physical laws, in other words. If you were able to bypass the infinity of this brane, the next one would likely be so very different that you would not survive."

"Good thing this one is infinite, then," I laughed. "Plenty to explore."

"Yes," Brian replied with a grin. "Sort of. Like I said, most of the realities sharing this brane with us are similar enough that you could live in any of them. Those closest would be virtually indistinguishable."

"Then how could we be sure they were actually different?" Jenna asked.

"You do the math." Brian finished his beer and set it down. "And if you have the computing power to make it happen, you can determine the degree of dislocation necessary to reach a reality within your brane that was truly different from your universe of origin."

"Wait," Mel said, holding up a hand. "Are you saying such travel is possible?"

"More than possible." Brian shrugged. "I'm doing so right now."

In the midst of a sea of conversation, our table was suddenly an island of self-conscious silence. We were surely all thinking the same thing, that this guy was one of those quiet whack jobs you sometimes encounter in life, and more often at a science fiction convention.

"Ah, no offense, but..." James began.

"Your skepticism does not offend me in the slightest," Brian assured him. "It's a perfectly reasonable response to such an outrageous assertion, for which there is no visible evidence." He shrugged. "Not yet, anyway."

"Not yet?" I repeated.

"If my calculations are correct, we're minutes away from the best possible proof," Brian replied. "You see, the picture book analogy – did I say metaphor the first time? Damn, I always mix those two up in conversation! Anyway, you all probably know what a 'signature' is, in book binding terms?"

"More properly called a 'section,'" Jenna said, nodding.

"Yes! You get it, then. The contents of a brane, we've discovered, are ordered in sections. The way the brane itself is filled with universes with very similar physical characteristics, a section or signature is a collection of universes that resemble each other to a high degree. But..." he paused as if for effect, sweeping his gaze around our little group. He seemed to be waxing enthusiastic, more so as he continued to hold forth.

And his accent became more pronounced, if not exactly identifiable.

"'But'..." Sylvia finally asked.

"Although there is an infinite number of signatures in each brane book, each signature itself contains a finite number of pages."

"That's - contradictory," Mel muttered.

"Reality so often is," Brian replied.

"So – this proof you mentioned," I said into a rather awkward silence. "It will take what form?"

"Well, if the calculations were correct, the energy that boosted me into this journey should take a certain amount of time to, ah, flip the right number of pages and send me into the next signature."

"How will you know?" Jenna asked.

"All the pages in this signature have elements in common." With a raised open hand, he gestured upward. "This building is not much different in form from the institute where I started the journey. I've passed through a steady set of alternates that had pretty much the same floor plan, but increasingly crowded functions. The last one was a college of some sort. Must have been near the start of a semester."

"How could you tell?" I asked.

"Lots of clueless people who looked a long way from home." Brian smirked. "I sort of fit in."

We were all playing along, and no doubt taking mental notes, by then. I mean, this was good stuff.

"What happens when you leave this section?" Jenna asked.

"Most of the commonalities will be lost. I'll be, for the first time, someplace fundamentally different from this."

"Okay, so this is, what? Some sort of recon mission?" I asked.

The wistful look was back. "Ah, no, it's a one-way trip, for me. And once I leave this signature, the remaining energy moving me along will be spent. Wherever I end up, that's where I live out my life!"

There was a moment of stunned silence. We were all quite caught up in this imaginative fabrication, and with the ease of its delivery. The man clearly believed every word he was saying.

"Good gawd, why would anyone do such a thing?" Mel demanded.

"Wanderlust?" Brian suggested. "Spirit of adventure?" He laughed a little and shook his head. "No, it's far more prosaic than that, my friends. I committed a murder, back at the lab. I killed the man who had stolen my life's work. A true crime of passion! And this is my grand escape."

The oddity in his voice had grown to the point that his words seemed – fuzzy. As if something distorted them. Or he was from Scotland.

"Murder?" Mel laughed openly; he clearly thought this was all ridiculous. "Damn, but this story gets better every minute."

"Yep, that's quite a tale…" James started to say.

There were only five people at the table.

"The fu – Where the hell…!" The words burst out of me.

Sylvia made a strangled squeak that would have been a scream if she'd had a moment to inhale. Jenna yelped in alarm. James and Mel were more efficient with their profanities than I'd been. People at nearby tables turned and stared; a few glared at us.

"Please tell me I just blinked – or something," said James.

"You didn't blink!" Sylvia said, eyes round. "We were all looking right at the man!"

"That didn't happen. Nope! It didn't!" Jenna sounded close to losing it.

"But it did," Mel said, gaping at the empty chair. "Goddam! We all saw it."

We exchanged bug-eyed stares, but no one said anything else. No one wanted to be the one to say it out loud, that the nice-looking whacko at our table had been telling the truth all the while. Jenna nodded and giggled in an alarming way. The silence at our table went on for a long time, until Sylvia suggested the bar across the street from the hotel, and nip of something stronger. The suggestion received no arguments. Hell, it wasn't even discussed. Sylvia and James flanked Jenna, still giggling, and herded her through the crowd. The rest of us followed, and believe me, we all had significantly more than a nip.

Our shared multiverse novel comes out next fall.

I wrote the part about the murderer.

EVIDENCE OF THINGS

They stepped out of the clinic, strolled to the corner and stopped.

"I'd forgotten the fair was this week," Reggie said, taking a look around. "That might explain the low attendance this morning."

"I've got the rest of the day free," Allen said, seeing an opportunity and seizing it. "Let's take a walk and see what's here this year."

"Sounds like a fine idea," Reggie said with a smile. "We'll finally have a chance to talk just the two of us."

They turned right, joining the crowd that filled the edges of the street, the center of which was occupied by a double row of canvas-walled booths.

It was late morning, but the breeze still carried a chilly touch, even though the clouds were gone and the bright winter sun lent a pleasant warmth when the air was still. A bright and beautiful morning in southern Arizona. Allen and Reggie strolled down the street, going with the flow. The world was bright and noisy. The smell of appetizing and unhealthy food being fried, grilled, and baked came to them every time the breeze was in their faces. They strolled past booths filled with various arts and crafts, and the people trying to sell it all.

"Before long," said Reggie, "I'm going to eat something I'll regret later."

"There was a food truck here last year," Allen said. "Most amazing sandwiches ever. Vietnamese, I think. I could eat a couple of those without slowing down!"

"Banh mi," Reggie said. "That's what you're talking about. Oh, I hope they're around here somewhere! Love those!"

Allen laughed and said, "I'll keep my eyes open."

"You have a nice laugh."

A bit startled, Allen said, "Really? Never thought of it that way before."

"Well, you do." Reggie smiled at him, a grin with nothing of shyness in it. "I don't think you ever laughed in the group."

"Not exactly a lot to laugh about." Allen shrugged and added, "I mean, support group for caregivers of the terminally ill?"

"You do hear laughter, though," she countered. "Sometimes. People trying to hold off the shadows by remembering better times."

Allen considered his experiences first as a group member, then as a volunteer counselor. "You're right. Guess I wasn't exactly the life of the party."

They walked a little further, then Reggie gave him a sidelong glance. "You're an inspiration."

Startled by the statement, Allen stopped and turned to face her. The crowd they'd kept pace with parted and flowed around them as if they were trees or lampposts. "Seriously? In what way?"

"You can't see it." Reggie shook her head and sighed. "But then, you wouldn't. Allen, you gave care and comfort to someone who really didn't deserve the best from you. By your own admission. But when she had no one else, you stepped in all the same. When people asked why you just shrugged and said it was the right thing to do."

"It was." Allen started walking again. "She really didn't have anyone else. Oh, that was her own damned fault, of course, but... Hell, Reg, no one deserved what happened to Beatrice. And no one should face that alone!"

"I fully agree," Reggie said. "That's why the support group is such a big part of my life. Those who take on such a task deserve all the help they can get."

"And I agree with that, which is why I volunteered to help out when, um, well, I was finished with what I needed to do."

"I did wonder why you stayed."

"That was part of the reason." Allen took a chance and slipped his hand into hers. She held on and didn't let go, but stopped walking and turned to face him again. Allen looked into blue eyes set in a pale face of gentle beauty, and brushed fine blond hair back when the breeze looped it around her chin. She closed her eyes for a moment as his fingertips stroked her cheek. Regina, a name she rarely answered to, was almost as tall as he was, and making eye contact was no challenge. The crowd once again flowed anonymously around them.

"I was hoping you'd say something like that, eventually," she said.

"I've developed a cautious nature, in that regard," he said. "I don't make connections as easily as I used to."

"Maybe so," Reggie said. "Some make them more easily than others. Too easily."

Allen shook his head. "It was a bad relationship. Really bad. So I have no idea why I felt so compelled to run to her the way I did. Something about that sort of, I don't know — scares me a little." He looked at her and saw in her eyes nothing but understanding. "Sometimes, it seems…"

"Seems like what, Allen?"

"Like I was made to do it." He looked away and started walking, but didn't let go of her hand.

They walked without speaking for a while, flowing with the crowd but oblivious to it. They paused and examined a booth filled with exquisite bonsai, watched over by a tall, heavy man who may or may not have had Japanese ancestry. After a few minutes they rejoined the crowd. The breeze flapped the canopy of the booth as they departed.

"That's possible, you know," Reggie said. "What you said about being made to help her. As if you weren't entirely acting of your own will."

"What do you mean?"

"What I said about connections, about how some make them more easily. Well, the flip side of that is that some are more open to those connections than others. People like you, who have an extraordinary amount of empathy."

"Empathy," Allen repeated.

"It's why you're so good with the others in the support group. You're – open. Receptive. I think Beatrice took advantage of that to draw you back to her."

"That makes no sense," Allen said, shaking his head. The street fair was just background noise by then. "She didn't contact me. I heard of her illness from a mutual friend. One of the few we had left, by then. Once I knew of it, I couldn't get it out of my mind."

"I didn't mean phone calls or emails," Reggie said. "When you started thinking about her it revived the connection you'd made with her years before. Then her need drew you. But don't blame her for that. The living do such things without being aware. Afterward, well, there's really no excuse."

"What are you talking about? Some sort of psychic coercion?" Allen took her silence for a positive answer, and laughed a bit ruefully. "Sorry, Reg, I don't go in for that sort of thing."

She glanced sidelong at him, with a gentle smile. "No unseen world behind the world for you, huh?"

"Not that I've ever seen credible evidence for, no," Allen replied. "I mean, I can't prove that such things don't exist, but I'm a bit beyond skeptical about them. So, no, I don't believe Beatrice drew me back because she had some sort of spiritual hold over me."

"And yet you said yourself that it seemed you were compelled?"

"Groping for words to explain emotions that I don't understand."

"Well, whatever you believe or don't believe, there are not many men like you in this world." She smiled at him and whatever worry the conversation caused Allen faded away. "Makes you worth saving, by my way of looking at it."

"Consider me saved," Allen said with a laugh.

"I get the feeling it's still a work in progress."

"I can live with that."

"So, you'll give me the same patience you showed toward those in the group? The seriously religious, I mean," she asked.

"I'm a thorough-going agnostic in matters supernatural," Allen admitted. "But I've never felt any need to be a jerk about. I mean, some of those people were losing, or had lost, someone they loved. They drew comfort and strength from those beliefs. So I tried to stay respectful. I'd be some kind of asshole, otherwise."

"Well, you are many things, my friend, but you are not an asshole."

"So, from all this I take it you believe in a god and that sort of thing?"

"Oh, I do indeed!" was Reggie's immediate response. "Not in ways that fit standard religions, but I do believe there's so much more to all of this than meets the eye!" And so saying, managed to somehow make a sweeping gesture that encompassed all the world around them, without decking anyone strolling along in the immediate vicinity. "And it's beautiful, how I see this reality. Oh, so beautiful!"

"If it works for you, that's fine by me," Allen said. "But I can't see it. I don't feel it. Until I have clear evidence that supports such a notion, I'll go on as I ever have. Keeping my mind and eyes open."

"Fair enough," she replied, putting her arm around him.

They walked on, looking at hats and homemade soap, sampling cheese, and passing comments back and forth, often with grins and the occasional chuckle. They bought nothing, but then, shopping wasn't why they were there. The street fair spread out into an intersection, and there they found the desired sandwiches. Drifting up the side street and away from the hubbub, they sat on the curb to eat. The noise of the fair reached them, but they had the spot to themselves. There was small talk, mostly about the food. Allen noticed that Reggie seemed to be inspecting the neighborhood around them, a collection of older houses, not all of them in good repair.

"Now, there we might find some of that evidence you need for things not seen," Reggie said, pointing to the house she meant with the straw in her iced tea.

"Madam Montovia?" Allen read aloud from the sign on the gate across from them. "Seriously? Crystal balls and tarot cards?" The images of the two items mentioned were drawn to either side of the sign's claim that Madam Montovia would know all and see all. For a modest fee.

"You never know what you'll find." She gave him a grin and a wink that seemed to mean she was joking about it all.

"Well, then, in the interest of open-minded research," said Allen, rising to his feet, and definitely of a mind to humor her, "let's see what there is to see, shall we?"

With a delighted laugh, Reggie took the hand he offered and stood. "You're humoring me, and I love you for it. And I'll make it worth your while, in the end."

That certainly sounded promising to Allen, even if he was embarrassed by being so obvious. They disposed of the trash left from their early lunch, passed through the gate and up a cracked concrete sidewalk flanked by ragged rose bushes. Reggie knocked on the door. After a brief pause they heard a variety of locks clicking and sliding open on the other side. The dark wooden door opened inward, and Allen was briefly disappointed that the hinges didn't squeak.

 The woman in the doorway had short, faded brown hair, and was neither especially heavy nor slim. She wore a long blue skirt that was decorated in haphazard fashion with stars and signs of the zodiac. Her blouse was green and made of something that attempted to imitate silk, with the faded look of a garment that has seen better days. She grinned at them, brown eyes in a round and slightly wrinkled face that Allen liked at once. "Welcome, my friends, to…" Madam Montovia began, obviously the first words of her routine. Then she let out a little squeak of surprise, her eyes suddenly round and wide.

 "Peace, sister," Regina said in a low, strangely commanding tone that startled Allen. "Have no fear. I have come seeking your aid."

 "I am honored, lady, and will do my best." She ducked her head once toward Reggie and indicated that they should follow her into the house. She looked Allen up and down, frowning. "Good heavens! And none too soon, I think."

 "Indeed," Reggie replied.

 "Say what?" Allen looked from one to the other, feeling completely adrift.

Reggie took him firmly by the hand and followed Madam Montovia, saying only, "You must trust me. Please."

Allen heard the sudden urgency in her voice and felt an immediate impulse to bolt, to flee to bright sunlight and cool breezes outside. The sandwich sat in his stomach like a ball of lead. And yet he followed Madam Montovia with Reggie at his side, clutching his hand. Neither the instinct to flee nor the steps he took into the house seemed of his own volition, as if he was suddenly the rope in a tug of war being pulled in opposite directions. Seeing the concern on her face tipped the balance; he stayed with Reggie.

Down a short, dim hallway, the walls of which were decorated with pictures he never really looked at, and into what would otherwise have been the master bedroom, to judge by its size. Cluttered sideboards lined two of the walls, and an assortment of ornate and padded chairs occupied the third. It was lit, barely, by fat candles in glass holders that were variously red, green or clear, and were tucked into the clutter of crystals, colored glass bottles, horned figurines, and bundles of leaves. A round table of dark wood, polished like a mirror, sat in the center of the room. Set in the center was a sphere of smooth crystal, perched on a golden tripod that was surrounded by branches cut from a shrub Allen didn't recognize. There was a light, fresh scent to the room from, he assumed, the candles.

There were three chairs at the table, spaced equally around it. Madam Montovia laid a hand on the back of one, caught Allen's eye and said, "Please, sit here."

Curiosity had replaced his moment of alarm, and Allen did as he was told. Madam Montovia took the chair to his left, and Reggie stepped around to the one on his right. She stood for a moment, and gave him a gentle smile. He was suddenly struck by how elegant she seemed, tall and slim and graceful. She had undone her hair when he was examining the room, and it hung about her shoulders and down her back, thick and pale.

Somehow her jeans and sweatshirt had been replaced by a loose white robe, belted at the waist. "Are you ready?" she asked the fortune teller.

"Yes, m'lady."

Reggie sat down and reached to either side, taking Allen's free hand in her left, and Madam Montovia's in her right.

"Reg – what's going on?" Allen asked.

"I said you were worth saving," she replied. "And the time has come."

Save me from what? He very much wanted to ask, but she was peering into the crystal ball and Montovia was murmuring words in a language Allen didn't recognize. There was a sensation of movement within the crystal that drew his eyes, as if a silver flame writhed within the ball. Almost as soon as he noticed this, pale light filled the thing and flashed out into the room.

He blinked against the brightness, and found himself in a place lit only by the crystal ball. The faces of the women on either side of him seemed suspended in darkness that pressed in from all sides. It was then that Allen noticed the lines of light coming out of him.

Two extended out through the darkness from his face, and it took a moment to realize that they came out of his eyes. Somehow, it didn't impair his vision, though it was no less alarming for that. Glancing down, he saw one extending from his chest, a couple of inches to the left of center. Another came from his naval. The last came from low on his groin, and that was more than a little frightening as well. Panic welled up in him, even as he realized there were no physical sensations associated with these lines of pale, white light. He made to stand up, but the women clutched his hands fiercely.

"Hold!" Regina commanded, and there was a quality to her voice that compelled obedience. "You are in no danger, Allen. Trust us. In the end, all will be made clear, I promise."

"She's coming!" Montovia gasped. "She's noticed us. She is coming for him, m'lady!"

The lines of light were suddenly pulled taut, and now there was both discomfort and terror; the very fear of death surged through him. He felt naked in the dark and wanted desperately to hide, but Allen could do nothing. Fear and bewilderment paralyzed him. His breath came in deep gasps and a deadly chill touched him where the lines of light emerged.

Allen felt something pulling at him, deep inside, and resisted the urge to move toward...

Beatrice!

For a moment she was right there, as plain as day, naked, a younger version of herself, still healthy and beautiful. Except for her eyes, which were black and empty pits. She reached out and gathered the lines of light in her hands. Where her hands touched the lines they became tarnished.

"I don't think so, bitch!" Regina snapped. "Now, sister! Hold him still!"

There was another pulse of light, and Allen felt everything about him go suddenly and unnaturally still. Regina was a looming presence, white and achingly beautiful, looming over the specter of his late ex-wife. Beatrice let go of the lines and faded into the darkness with a wailing shriek. From her side Regina drew a short golden sword that sparkled and emitted a high keening sound as she raised it high. She swept the weapon down in a smooth, short arc that cut through the lines of light. And the lines parted, writhing for a moment before fading into the darkness.

Which wasn't darkness any more.

They were in the room, lit by candles. Madam Montovia let go a sigh and slumped in her chair as if exhausted, while Reggie – in jeans and a sweatshirt once more – regarded him with a look of concern. "Allen? Are you okay? How do you feel?"

"Tired," he replied, using the first word to come to him as he tried to get a grip on the strange mix of feelings he endured; fear, loss, anger, grief, confusion, along with a sense of being drained and strangely disoriented, as if he'd suddenly lost his sense of direction. "What the hell was that?" he demanded, appalled that his voice shook as it did.

"That was evidence of things normally unseen."

"Seriously, Reggie, what just happened?"

"I cut you free," she replied.

"From what?" He held her gaze for a moment. "Beatrice? That was really...?"

Reggie nodded once. "I told you before that you're a man endowed with an extraordinary degree of empathy. Unfortunately, that makes you vulnerable to a greedy spirit such as the one that was, in this world, your ex-wife. That's why you went back to her in the end. Those connections you saw, it's how she was able to cling to you and summon you back."

"She was trying to come back from the dead?" Allen guessed, barely able to believe he was saying such words.

"No," said Madam Montovia, looking tired and old, and a little sad. "She was afraid, and wanted to take you with her so she wouldn't be alone."

Allen stared at the now quiet crystal ball, considered what had just been said, and what it surely meant. Or would have meant, if...

"Damn," he whispered, suddenly shaking with anger.

"In life, she knew nothing of what she did," Reggie assured him. "But in death, well, when we leave this world for a time, things are laid bare. Some are less graceful with these revelations than others."

"He should be outside, now, m'lady," Montovia said. "Out in the sun and wind and the living world."

"Yes, indeed." Reggie stood up and gave the other woman a fond smile. "Thank you for grounding us, sister. I am in your debt."

"Not at all," Montovia said as she rose to her feet and bowed her head. "It was an honor to be of assistance."

Reggie led Allen out, back into the light of day, where they found the breeze had picked up. The air was brisk and fresh. They stood facing each other a few steps away from the front door. "A host of questions," she said, smiling. "I can see them in your eyes."

"What am I supposed to believe? And why do I feel so – lost, all of a sudden?"

"You'll believe what your heart and mind know to be true." Reggie laughed quietly as she reached out to take his hands in hers. "And now, you have the time ahead of you in which to sort this out. I will help you, there. As for feeling lost, you were connected to Beatrice for a long time. Freedom will take a little getting used to." The look of concern returned. "I did what I did because Madam Montovia is right. You are a good man. I could not let Beatrice drag you from this world before your time!"

"So – what are you, exactly? Some kind of guardian angel?"

A quirky smile touched her lips, and Reggie put her arms around him and pulled him close. Allen felt no need to resist. "A guardian of sorts, yes," she said, half an inch from kissing him. "But I'm no angel!"

She gave him ample evidence, then, that she spoke the truth.

An excerpt from ***The Luck of Han'anga***
War of the Second Iteration, Book One

"The trap in which you played an unwitting role was laid many months before your probe came into this system. We knew a large scale offensive was in the planning stages, an attempt by the current rulers of the Republic to divert their people from their own internal divisions. We ordered our defenses to direct the offensive to this part of the Confederation, in an attempt to bring forces of the Republic as close to the point of contact between the Commonwealth and Confederation space as we could. You see, my friends," and his gaze swept the room as he spoke, "we already knew you were out there, and that contact between the Commonwealth and the Confederation of Clans was imminent."

The room was stunned into silence. No one even shifted in a chair. Then, finally, Moresh said, "You set us up from the very beginning."

"Yes," Kr'nai Ersha said quietly.

"How long have you been aware of the Commonwealth?" Sadov demanded.

"For almost three of your years," the Leyra'an replied. "The system you name Eriola is actually within what we consider Confederation space. It has been our habit for many years now to quietly investigate new systems without actually sending ships, in case the Republic was there first. This time we spotted your probeship, instead. We have monitored the settlement of Eriola since then, withdrawing only when you started using the other node. This was only the first such encounter. We have quietly withdrawn from several systems, since then, in the hope that you would continue to expand into this sector. And you did."

"Why not simply contact us, and ask for help?" Moresh demanded.

"I was unable to convince the Clan Councils of the wisdom of such a plan. In fact, I was forbidden to reveal our presence," Kr'nai Ersha replied. "So, with the help of those who support me out here on the frontier, I made it impossible for the three civilizations to *avoid* contact. We fell back in a way that led the Republic through sparsely-settled systems and into this sector, and when your probe arrived here, we let the route to Pr'pri system become the path of least resistance." He lowered his gaze to the table with a sigh. "There was never a very firm plan, of course. How could there be? So much was left to chance, and chance very nearly undid us."

"We're listening," Moresh prompted when he fell silent.

"The fighting went badly for us. The systems under assault did not fall to the Republic in the order we expected, and a planned line of escape for refugees was lost, sending them all here, where the trap was set. We tried, oh how we tried, to get everyone away from here, before it was too late!"

"Everyone?" Moresh asked coldly.

"I speak only of our own people," Kr'nai

Ersha admitted. "Your presence in this system was, of course, essential. From my studies of Human history, or rather, that of the Republic, I knew they harbored certain fears concerning the Humanity their ancestors left behind. I also know that a great many citizens of the Republic have prayed for the day of reunion, hoping for reconciliation with the people their forefathers abandoned. No matter which opinion was held by the commander of the attacking fleet, and I *did not know* Andrew Kester would lead the inevitable assault, I believed the reunion, happening here, would be too great a surprise to allow them to follow through on their battle plan."

"You were wrong," said Moresh.

"And I acknowledged such a possibility, to myself at least," Kr'nai Ersha replied. "This is why the fleet remained concealed the entire time you were here. I could not help the fear that whoever commanded the Republic's fleet would refuse to believe you, and so I made ready a back-up plan, which in the end was the plan I used. That particular deception was as much for your protection as any..."

"They think we are on your side," Moresh said in a low voice, the tone of which seemed to lower the temperature of the room.

Robert studied his Captain closely, his heart beating so hard he felt the pulse clearly in his throat. This was not the woman he had known for so many years. She could be hard, he knew, as well as uncompromising. But he had never seen in her such a capacity for rage, and anything but a cold rage, as it turned out.

"In time they will..." Kr'nai Ersha began.

"They think we've taken sides, damn you!" And her right hand slammed down sharply on the tabletop.

Robert jumped in his seat at the hard sound, and was aware that everyone around him flinched and blinked, as if evading a blow. He had never heard Captain Moresh raise her voice in such a way, much less provide a visible demonstration of anger. Even the Leyra'an flinched, almost in unison. Robert found that he had clenched his fists, and with an effort relaxed them.

"You want us to mediate an end to this war of yours," Sadov said more quietly. "To do that it is *essential* we appear neutral. You have badly and *deeply* compromised that neutrality!"

"Only for the short term, I am sure," Kr'nai Ersha insisted. "Yes, we hope you can bring peace, but I cannot ask my leaders, my people, to begin negotiations while the Republic is actively invading the Confederation of Clans! I needed you here to stop their advance."

"Did you ever send the message we prepared for the Republic?" Sadov demanded.

"Yes, but apparently they did not take it seriously," Kr'nai Ersha replied.

"If they had done so," his niece added, "none of this would have happened."

"Gaia," and Sadov rubbed at his temples as if in pain.

"You should have abandoned your plan,"

Moresh said in a voice that returned to a normal volume, but remained frigid in tone. "If not for us, then for the sake of those ships by the node that you *knew* could not defend themselves. Or did you feel the need to motivate us?"

Robert braced himself for furious denials from the Leyra'an, but though Kr'nai Ersha stiffened and clenched his fists, teeth flashing for a moment into clear view, he made no reply. It was Kr'nai Melep who spoke, meeting the Captain's anger eye to eye without flinching. "We had watchers posted," she said softly. "They were to warn us of any fleet movements toward the node in Arla'not System. We should have had time to move the ships back. The watchers failed us, which means they are dead. The loss of so many ships was *not* a part of our plan!"

"Nor did we expect the Republic to attack unarmed ships," Kr'nai Ersha said bitterly, his eyes directed toward the table. "This they have not done before, and is why we used ships in disguise," he added with bitter irony. He looked up at Moresh, eyes flashing with emotion, wet with tears. "You have no idea how that felt, to see my calculated deception take those innocent lives. To stand on your ship and watch my people die and be able to do *nothing!*" His voice had an odd, strangled catch to it. He paused and seemed to hold his breath for a moment as if fighting for self-control. "I wanted to kill them, the invading ships," he went on darkly. "I wanted to watch them *die!*

And I had at hand," and he stretched out his right hand toward the Captain, "the power to utterly wipe them out!" Now he was meeting the Captain's eyes and he clenched that hand into a fist as he nearly shouted the words at her. When he continued his voice was harsh and broken, a struggle to push words through powerful emotions. "But even more I want this all to *end!* Can you not see?" He looked around at those assembled, eyes glittering. "*It must end!* And to accomplish this I will do whatever I must. *Use* whatever I must." The upraised arm dropped to his side. "My apologies I reserve for my own people. Those who paid the price, and those who must now grieve."

An excerpt from *The Gryphon Stone*

We climbed into the hills soon after. The tallest shoulders of stone looked over the roundabout, down and past ranks of outcrops and boulders through which the stream tumbled before it flowed into a small lake. By then we'd changed into spare clothes; the condition of those we'd cleaned did not pass muster with Mistress Malley, who took them in hand. We wore our swords and great coats, and I carried a pair of blankets for sitting. These were all the comforts Island tradition allowed. We'd eaten a light supper, but brought no food or water with us. I could feel the eyes of our fellow travelers follow us up the slope. Word had spread; they knew where we went, and they knew why. This was made clear by so many of them making the sign of the Two, as we passed by.

Sid picked a flat boulder perched at the top of the hill and, as the sun slipped below the horizon, we climbed onto it. At that high point we arranged the blankets and stood facing each other. "Our blades will lie between us, unsheathed," she said, drawing hers. "They must not touch. We will sit back-to-back, and we will not touch or speak or look upon one another until you see the sun rise. When it clears the horizon, you will tell me the vigil has ended."

"Got it," I said. I drew my sword, and it caught a gleam of red light from the fading sunset. It was completely quiescent in my hand. I could only hope the same was true of Sid's weapon. We set them down, side by side, hers pointing south, mine north. Sid turned to face the sunset, and I followed her gaze.

How recently had we watched that fierce red glow fade in the west, and not long after made love beneath the stars? And now we would keep a vigil beneath those same stars, as my lover sought absolution from deities I didn't even believe in. The strangeness and frightful beauty of this life I've led never ceases to amaze me. I suppose, on balance, that's a good thing.

As the sky darkened overhead, Sid started to sing a hymn in the language of the Islands. I didn't know the language then, but the pleading sound of her voice, and the tears I could hear beneath it, made my heart ache. All the more so, knowing there was nothing I could do. The hymn went on and on, with short pauses for breath. I didn't dare so much as take her hand in mine. It wasn't just that she'd told me not to touch her. It *felt* like the wrong thing to do.

Only a dark band of blue remained above the western horizon as the song ended, and Sid indicated that we should sit. I did so, facing east, Sid at my back, both of us wrapped in coats. I settled in for a long night.

It was a very long night indeed.

I've kept long watches, in my day, and gone without sleep more times than I care to count. But I'd never done anything quite like this before. Knowing where my friend's head was at, what she had to be feeling, and yet not really understanding what she was about – I'm a thorough-going agnostic in such matters – all sorts of thoughts floated through my mind. The stars slowly turned from east to west over the wide, shadowy landscape around us. The sounds of the camp below died away and there was only the whisper of a light breeze sighing over the rocks, the chatter of the stream pouring over the stones of its narrow bed, and a single loud and persistent cricket that I swore I would one day hunt down and kill.

    The air grew chilly, and I pulled the collar of my coat up around my neck. Sid sat behind me, as still as the stone beneath us. My mind wandered, and I found myself reliving snatches of memory. The dragons on the Golden Gate Bridge, the Moj hordes appearing in North Carolina and Texas, and kaiju rising from the sea. I remembered the day the Alvehn came and saved us from the Moj. I remembered fighting in the unit of militia my father formed when the black drakes appeared. I recalled his death, sometime later, as we fought the Moj. For not the first time, I took comfort in the knowledge that his sacrifice had saved a city. I looked back at many of my experiences, that night, the beauty and love, the horror and grief, and the sheer wonder of the multiverse. It defies my meager skill with words.

    I remained awake and at her back all through her vigil. Instead of falling asleep, I seemed to enter a strange sort of mental state that was neither wakeful nor unconscious. It was awareness and feeling only, without thought. My wandering recollections faded away. I was aware of the quiet night, and of the woman who sat behind me. Acutely aware of Sidraytha. Somehow, though we faced away from each other, I knew she remained awake. Time became a single, eternal moment; reality was as crystal clear as the stars overhead.

The sky was growing pale to the east. I watched as the stars faded and the thin, pale crescent of the old moon rose ahead of the dawn. Birds called out to each other in shrill, bubbling whistles from the shadowy land around us. The sky grew steadily brighter and more birds joined that dawn chorus. It seemed to take forever, but at last a fiery sliver of light burst over the rim of the world. In a moment it was too bright to look at directly, and in the fullness of time, the sun rose above the horizon. The vigil had ended.

Feeling stiff and a little shaky, I got my knees under me and turned toward Sid. "It's done," I said. I looked up into the sky, stretching my back, and saw gryphons circling overhead. They were still watching us. I had no problem with that, not after what had happened.

Sid let go a deep sigh and bent forward a little, then nodded. "It is done," she agreed, and though she needed no assistance, accepted my hand as I helped her stand.

"Are you okay?" I asked.

"Yes," she said with another nod. "It would seem the God and Goddess share your judgment of me, Daffyd." And she smiled, then stepped forward and kissed me. It was a brief kiss, and after it we just stood there, holding each other for a moment as the day brightened around us.

I saw our companions just as she turned from me, and knew she did so as well when she let out a little gasp of surprise. There, on the rocks below us, with lanterns and candles and green glow lights that all still gleamed or flickered in the shadows cast by the hill, were what appeared to be most of the caravan's company. Closest were Korl, Tensta, and Trey; arrayed around them were most of the surviving caravan guards. Not far down the hill I saw Grevin, the Prince, and the rest of the players. Master and Mistress Malley stood close together, holding hands. Beyond them, the rocks were liberally sprinkled with people, looking up at us. All of them looked utterly exhausted.

Our fellow travelers, aware of what Sid needed to do, and why, had chosen to keep the watch with me.

Sid stared out over them for a moment, speechless, then as tears spilled from her eyes she made the sign of the Two over them. After that, she went down on one knee and bowed her head.

I knelt beside her, and did the same.

About the author...

I am a writer and science fiction fan based in Tucson, Arizona, with a background in botany (B.S. Plant Sciences, University of Arizona) and a passion for astronomy. In my spare time I study history, nature, and any other subject that holds still long enough for me to get a good look at it.

Made in the USA
Monee, IL
17 October 2024

67982617R00049